MY LOVE AND THANK YOU WITH KISSES TO
MY WIFE, MEE KYUNG, AND OUR TWO LOVELY
DAUGHTERS, SUNG AND HEE EUN. I HOPE THESE
SANTA BOOKS HLEP KIDS EVERYWHERE READ
BETTER AND SMILE MORE OFTEN.

DONG H. CHUNG
NOVEL UNIVERSE LLC

STONE AGE Santa

BY KEVIN O'DONNELL

ILLUSTRATED BY BOO YOUNG KIM & DAVID HEO

g

GRAPHEDIA

ATHENS, GEORGIA

GRAPHEDIA BOOKS

Published in the United States of America by

Hill Street Press LLC | 191 East Broad Street
Suite 216 / Athens, Georgia 30601

www.hillstreetpress.com

Published in an alliance between:

Hill Street Press LLC (Thomas Payton)
Novel Universe LLC (Edward Kim), and
Seoul Movie Co., Ltd. (Chang Rok, Jeon)

Book and cover composition by Jenifer Carter.
Manufactured in the USA.

Library of Congress Control Number:

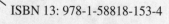

ISBN 13: 978-1-58818-153-4

First Printing

10 9 8 7 6 5 4 3 2 1

WARNING: DO NOT ATTEMPT ANY OF THE STUNTS IN THIS BOOK. A MAGICAL FLYING SLEIGH IS NOTHING TO FOOL WITH. RUDOLPH AND THE OTHER REINDEER ARE HIGHLY TRAINED PROFESSIONALS WHILE SANTA, THOUGH UTTERLY UNTRAINED, IS FILLED WITH GOBS OF CHRISTMAS SPIRIT. WE'RE EXPECTING ALL OF THEM TO MAKE IT THROUGH THE ENTIRE BOOK. IN THE OUTLINE EVERYBODY DOES JUST FINE, THOUGH IT DOES GET A LITTLE STICKY NEAR THE END. IN ANY EVENT, WE ARE PROUD TO PRESENT STONE AGE SANTA.
PS. NO REFUNDS!!!

With Christmas but one week away, Santa is hurrying home to the North Pole when, unbeknownst to him, the sinister corporate jet of an even more sinister company owned by the super sinister Mr. Horrible cruises up behind him.

Santa is about to burst into song, over the objections of his team of trusty reindeer (Yes, there are only four reindeer for that is all Santa takes on pre-Christmas maintenace flights.) But, before he can get the first words out of his mouth he is hit by a barrage of . . .

. . . Snowballs! Caught totally by surprise, Rudolph and his team are unable to pull the sleigh out of range and within moments they are spiraling out of control down towards what promises to be a horrendous crash landing.

While Mr. Horrible gloats back in his headquarters, Santa and his reindeer plummet ever closer to the unmapped and presumably deserted island far below.

While Rudolph and the other reindeer strug-
gled to gain control, Santa . . . well, Santa
yelled "Wheeeeeeeee" as loud as he could.

Drawing on his Special Forces reindeer training, Rudolph takes control of the situation and calls for the team to try a daring maneuver that could just possibly save their lives and Christmas.

Recognizing that no one could ever recover from such a dive, Mr. Mucky slows down and reports back to Mr. Horrible at headquarters. Victory!

Incredibly, an explosion erupts from the island below and, even more incredibly, Santa and Rudolph can't be seen or heard any more.

Back in his office, Mr. Horrible savors the moment. With Santa gone his Horrible toy empire can only grow.

THE PUBLISHER WOULD LIKE TO APOLOGIZE FOR THE SUDDEN AND DRAMATIC LOSS OF SANTA CLAUS. WE REGRET THIS UNFORTUNATE OCCURRENCE HOWEVER IF YOU WILL REFER BACK TO THE FIRST PAGE YOU WILL RECALL THAT THERE ARE

NO REFUNDS.

THE REST OF THE BOOK WILL BE · · · WELL · · · BLANK!

And we're back. It turns out that Rudolph's roll saved everyone's life. The sleigh though was in ruins and would require some nifty carpentry work; something that Santa was not good at. Not good at all.

At this point, having been born with over-active sweat glands and an ironic aversion to wool, Santa slipped out of his holiday suit and into something pretty close to his birthday suit.

WRITE YOUR OWN VERSE:

_____

_____

_____

WRITE YOUR OWN VERSE:

_____

_____

_____

In a nearby valley three cave kids couldn't help but hear Santa's singing. Woopy, a bright cautious cave girl with golden hair was the first to hear it.

Choo Choo, who always wore a skull mask on his head for absolutely no apparent reason, covered his ears while Ding Dong, a young genius - it is rumored that he can count to five - correctly identifies Santa's singing as the sounds of a man.

And so Santa stood in the center of the forest and wondered where he could find some wood to build his sleigh with. Luckily, at that moment Woopy, Choo Choo, and Ding Dong arrived.

Showing a surprising lack of perception, Santa at first mistakes the cave kids for elves but is quickly corrected.

Following standard cave kid protocol, Woopy proposes that they capture the strange looking foreigner, tie him on a stake and take him to the village so the Chief can decide what to do with him.

After the cave kids tie Santa up to a pole and start to carry him back to their village, Santa opens his mouth and confirms that he may indeed be nutty by breaking out into a song. A very loud song, sung very off key.

At the same time that Santa was being carted away by the cave kids (who were wishing they had bad hearing), Mr. Mucky was landing his jet at the South Pole.

Horrible Toys opened their South Pole factory when Mr. Horrible discovered that penguins would work for seaweed. Today, it is second only to Santa's workshop in toy production and first in over-worked penguins who are very tired of seaweed.

By now you may have undoubtedly picked up on the fact that Mr. Horrible is, well . . . horrible. Some attribute this to a lack of nurturing hugs, during his youth, caused by . . .

. . . his mother's Aggressive Flatulence Syndrome, or AFS, which kept all humans, including her children, ten to fifteen feet away at all times.

In an ironic twist of design, Santa's North
Pole workshop made liberal use of the sadly
underutilized but always proud penguin motif.

Let's cut to the bottom line, Elfy. Santa's dead, so your toys are worthless! But I'll buy them, for pennies on the dollar, so you can learn what Christmas is really all about . . . PROFITS! Ha ha ha ha!

Mr. Horrible you're a twit, Santa is fine. If he wasn't, the Santa lights would go out. But, as you can see, they're shining as bright as ever.

Santa's head elf was a feisty little guy who enjoyed nothing more than sending Mr. Horrible into a stressed out, eye popping, hissy fit.

Mr. Horrible turned to look just as the giant penguin eyes, otherwise known as the Santa Lights, shone as bright as any giant penguin eyes have ever shone.

Immersed in a full blown hissy fit, Mr. Horrible
commanded Mr. Mucky back to the jet. In
the meantime Santa's head elf had a private
gleeful moment that can best be described as
"scrumptuous."

Back in the village Chief Ugga looked at his latest captive with pride. If the bone going through his head had not damaged his niceness lobe he would have even thanked the three little cave kids that caught him.

Santa, who was always comfortable just hanging out, was still as jolly as ever. Of course the sudden news that you are about to be eaten by cannibals can put a bit of a damper on anybody's spirit, even Santa's.

The cave kids were starting to feel bad that they
had brought the jolly man with the red hat back
to their village. Very few children like to think
they're responsible for someone being eaten.

Santa was not about to let a little bad voodoo prevent him from keeping himself alive. Even as he spoke to his new little cave kid captors, he was devising a brilliant escape plan.

Well, Santa was devising at least half of a brilliant escape plan. He had forgotten about his feet and the chances of Santa untying them on his own were not very good.

Even so, Santa's everlasting confidence in kids was soon rewarded. The brave little cave kids realized that they couldn't let their new strange, but lovable, friend end up as that night's buffet.

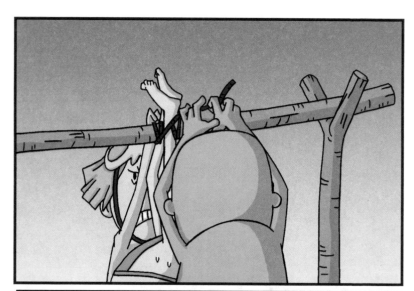

So Choo Choo and Ding Dong swiftly untied Santa's feet, just as Woopy spotted the chief headed their way, along with the village's biggest busybody . . . and we do mean biggest.

Madame Yum Yum was the president of the Cave Woman's Auxiliary League. As such, she controlled the biggest voting block in village elections and she made sure Chief Ugga knew it.

Before Chief Ugga knew what was going on, Santa and his three new best friends raced off into the forest. Though Santa was a hefty heifer, he was filled with so much Christmas Spirit that he zipped right along and prepared to burst into song.

Chief Ugga and Madame Yum Yum watched in frustration as the chubby man in the red hat ran along, with the gall to start singing a song.

The Chief yelled out for his assistant, Major Dum Dum, a cave man who had risen steadily through the village civil service program to reach his current position where he was next in line to be interim chief, if needed.

Wanting nothing more than to be chief . . .
Major Dum Dum was constantly trying to get
his Dino Flyer to drop a big boulder on the
Chief's head and kill him. This made the
chief mad.

Major Dum Dum was very organized. When he wasn't busy trying to get the chief squashed by a giant boulder, he was busy with his work . . . like catching people with dinosaur dogs.

MEANWHILE

Faster Mr. Mucky! We've got to get down to that island and finish Santa off fast, so I can make it back in time for my bi-weekly bananafana facial.

Yes sir, Mr. Horrible. I've got the new Robo Smacker 2008 ready to go in with us. That thing will catch and crush him in no time.

Good, because if I don't foliate my skin enough, I'm a wreck!

Inside the Horrible Toys jet, Mr. Mucky steered for the remote island where Santa had crashed. In the plane they had packed their most dangerous toy; the Robo Smacker 2008 ... a real "Smacker of a Robot."

ROBO SMACKER 2008

BIGGEST CLAWS ON THE MARKET

The Robo Smacker 2008 was the crowning achievement of Horrible Toys' horrible laboratory. It had the actual capacity to do great damage and for this feature Mr. Horrible charged extra.

AVAILABLE WITH SECRET
POWERFUL BOOTY LASER*

1 MILE

BOOM

*assembly and special upgrade kit required

The special booty laser beam tested out as
EXCELLENT up to one mile in distance. It
could sear through a two inch thick metal
door in five seconds and was outlawed in 42
countries.

So, as Mr. Horrible boarded his jet and plotted his revenge upon Santa, the portly Saint Nick was traipsing along, singing in the woods. Choo Choo and Woopy tried to silence him but to no avail.

The first sharp howls of the dino dogs leapt out behind the four travelers and the gravity of the situation grew. If the dino dogs got hold of them they would be goners. They had to get to the river . . . quick!

Flush with the thought of taking a white-water dip, Santa instantly pointed out the fact that he was river-ready and then started thinking of another trampling sing-along-song.

Hmmm . . . before we start to sing along on the song about the thong with Woopy, Choo Choo, and Ding Dong, this is probably a good moment to recap our situation.

After having been shot down by a barrage of snowballs, Santa was captured by three cave kids and carried to the village. There, the Chief promised him as dinner for Madame Yum Yum only to have Santa escape with the aid of Woopy, Choo Choo, and Ding Dong and run away to the forest. Major Dum Dum was assigned to track Santa down with a pack of wild and ravenous dinosaur dogs. Santa's incessant singing helped put the dino dogs on their trail. Now, in an effort to evade them they are heading towards a river where they can hide their tracks. They hope. And now, the song to sing along on: the Sing-a-Long Thong Song.

SUBMIT YOUR OWN LYRICS AT WWW.STONEAGESANTA. COM AND THE FAVORITES WILL BE PICKED TO BE PUT ONLINE FOR EVERYONE TO SEE.

MY THONG SONG

We got idea. You like thong. It OK we go to water now?

After you little cave kid genius. But I am excited to see one of these dino dogs. They sound cute.

Santa was sadly mistaken, For in reality dino dogs are anything but cute. Their mothers know they're ugly and give them bags to put over their heads at the dinner table. The extra nostril holes right in their forehead make a sneeze potentially lethal.

DINO DOGS
Voted World's Uncutest Creature

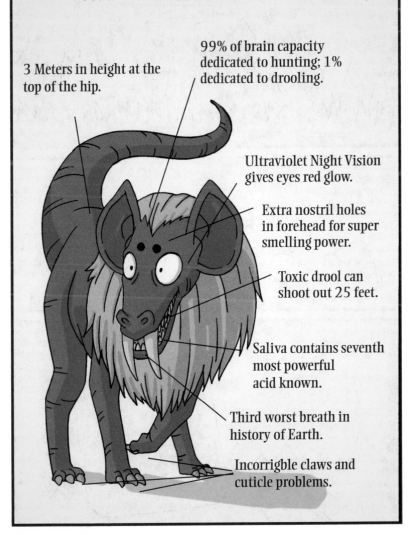

3 Meters in height at the top of the hip.

99% of brain capacity dedicated to hunting; 1% dedicated to drooling.

Ultraviolet Night Vision gives eyes red glow.

Extra nostril holes in forehead for super smelling power.

Toxic drool can shoot out 25 feet.

Saliva contains seventh most powerful acid known.

Third worst breath in history of Earth.

Incorrigble claws and cuticle problems.

NAME THE DINO DOGS: SUMBIT YOUR NAMES AT WWW.STONEAGESANTA.COM.

Though the Dino Dogs had heard Santa singing, the canyons made for strange echoes. So, they still needed to pick up his scent and they sniffed at the air with their four hungry nostrils.

Inspired by Major Dum Dum's offer, the dino dogs sniffed and whiffed until they had picked up the scent and shot off at full speed, pulling Major Dum Dum along behind them.

Transportation corridor located. Scanning for Santa cells in atmosphere.

It's about time! These plants are dirty with bugs. It's not like Antarctica. There it's just me and the penguins. I love those penguins. They're better than elves. Oh, who am I kidding? Of course the elves are better. That's why kids like Santa's toys more than mine.

On the other side of the river the Robo Smacker 2008 cut a path out of the forest up to a cliff overlooking the water. Since they had lowered it to the island, the robot had been scanning for tell tale molecules matching Santa's DNA.

The air above the river channel, which the robot called a transportation corridor, was carrying Santa cells and the Robo Smacker 2008 didn't miss them. Nor did it miss the opportunity to clarify why kids prefer Santa's toys.

In that moment Mr. Horrible revealed his vulnerable side and when Mr. Mucky handed him a tissue he suddenly broke down. And for one glorious moment of Mr. Mucky's life he was appreciated by Mr. Horrible.

At first, Mr. Mucky couldn't believe his ears. After years of dedicated and thankless service to this ingenious, though demented, boss, he was about to be rewarded and then . . . not so much.

"Now, that's how you dispose of a tissue."

Ruing the fact that his moment of retribution had been ruined by Mr. Horrible's obsession with overzealous tissue disposal protocol, Mr. Mucky proceeded to evaporate the offensive clump.

Though it revealed one of millions of character flaws that Mr. Horrible possessed, you have to be impressed with how effectively that tissue was disposed of. Meanwhile, Robo Smacker 2008 prepared to catch Santa.

It turns out that while the river was good at hiding tracks, it put Santa and the cave kids right smack in the middle of Mega-Carp central. Danger lurked on all sides while Santa blew bubbles.

Just as Ding Dong had predicted with forlorn certitude a massive mega-carp leapt up out of the river and opened its mouth in anticipation of scrunching down on the furry little person named Santa that it wanted to eat . . . really bad.

With great dexterity, Santa twirled in the air and landed with his feet on the Mega Carp's bottom teeth and a little stick pushing the upper jaw open just long enough to grab a passing peace of driftwood and slam it into place making it imposible for the fish to close its mouth.

At the sound of the dino dogs Santa forgot his speech and leapt into the water, leaving a dazed and very anti-Santa mega-carp in his wake. Even though Santa looked chubby and chewy, none of the mega-carp wanted to even get close to this crazy man.

Though he knew Santa was correct in diving into
the river and swimming away from the approaching
dino dogs, Ding Dong could not help but wonder
if the strange man who had fallen from the sky
was ready to be committed to the witch doctor's
crazy cave?

On the shore Major Dum Dum released his hounds and as soon as they started racing up the shore he pulled out his trusty and ever present TO DO list. He had always been and would always remain a very organized cave man.

As the cave kids floated and swam down the river with Santa, their predicament looked horribly bleak. Dino Dogs were on the shore and Mega-Carp were in the river. They had no where to go . . . until Ding Dong got an idea.

And with that Ding Dong stood up and proceeded to taunt the Dino Dogs mercilessly. Well, in short order they were so inflamed they leapt in and charged through the Mega-Carp infested waters.

Well, just as Ding Dong had expected, the moment before the Dino Dogs were about to reach them, a Mega-Carp leapt out of the water and commenced to try and eat all three Dino Dogs at once.

The Dino Dogs lurched out of the jaws of the Mega-Carp and raced back up the shore at full speed which resulted in the "To Do" list reading, unsuspecting Major Dum Dum being run over . . . twice.

With the Mega-Carp and Dino Dogs momentarily disposed of, Santa spied a grove of trees that he could use to build his sleigh. They were right next to the shore where the Robo Smacker 2008 was standing.

Yes, much to the shock of many of those floating on the log, the Robo Smacker 2008 stood on the shore with its massive, powerful multi tasking claws pointing back out at them as they drew nearer by the moment.

Time out. Why robot on shore? By way, what is robot? Choo Choo, and how you know it named "robot"?

Mr. Horrible, we have visual on Santa.

I'll take it from here. . . . Ahoy, Santa . . . or, I'm sorry, Saint Nick! I forgot, you're A SAINT? Hah! Well you can't run a profitable business on Christmas spirit alone, buddy. With you gone I'll ship in a few penguins, crush the elf union and, bingo bongo, I'll be richer than ever. Of course, with you in my commercials, I'd make even more money. Last chance, Santa, wanna be partners? I'm making myself vulnerable here. Don't hurt me.

Even though Mr. Horrible wanted Santa to stop living as soon as possible, he wanted to make more money . . . even more. So, though he loathed his very sight, Mr. Horrible offered Santa a chance to be partners.

Santa turned Mr. Horrible down in as quick and jolly a manner as anyone really could. Even so, the hyper-sensitive toy tycoon got his feelings hurt.

Ooh, that's a better plan. HEY Santa. Prepare to have your head crushed in my Robot's giant claws. Ha Ha Ha.

Ho Ho Ho, that is an impressive robot. Kudos to your penguins! So I guess his claws shoot way out so I can't just float past him, right?

Quickly deserting his sulking strategy, Mr. Horrible yelled at Santa, telling him that his head was about to be crushed in the claws of his robot. True to form, Mr. Horrible's warning had no effect on Santa.

Saved by Mr. Horrible's penchant for penny pinching in development and production, Santa and the cave kids were seemingly immune from any of the Robo Smacker 2008's powers. Except, that is, for one . . .

Unbeknownst to anyone at Horrible Toys, two renegade hacker penguins had written a special teletransport program into the chip inside the Robo Smacker 2008. With the push of a button, Mr. Horrible and Mr. Muchky were teletransported up to their jet.

Back up in his plane, mr. Horrible immediately fired a horrible missile down at Santa and the cave kids just as they were stepping onto the opposite shore of the river.

Not knowing how Mr. Horrible had managed to get up into his plane, Santa saw the missile at the last second and yelled for the cave kids to jump for their lives. All four of them flew into the air just before the missile crashed into the ground beside them.

With Santa, once again, seemingly blasted to smithereeens, Mr. Horrible put on his favorite virtual reality helmet and ordered the concerned and subservient Mr. Mucky back to the South Pole.

As improbable as it seems, Santa and the cave kids survived yet again. Santa's indominatable Christmas spirit and the quick reflexes of the cave kids saved them.

YEP, HE'S STILL ALIVE AND SINGING TO THE TUNE OF "HARK THE HERALD, ANGELS SING."

Hark the Herald, Angels sing . . .
I'm just happy that we're living.
We're dirty and my ears ring . . .
But I don't care because I'm living.

If you're worried because of school . . .
Or some kids don't think you're cool . . .
Just do what I do every day . . .
Thank God you're alive and play, play, play

Hark the Herald, Angels sing.
We're just glad that we're living!

As the skies cleared and everything looked rosy, Santa broke into song. This time, the mood was so infectious that the cave kids zipped right into a quick conga line behind Santa and joined in.

Once the singing was over Santa did one of his patented one-handed handstands and, with Ding Dong itching to get going, they turned their attention to building a sleigh.

Back in the village, Major Dum Dum's news was eagerly awaited by the Chief who instantly started grilling his assistant when he saw him arrive empty handed.

Before the Chief could finish balling out Major Dum Dum and then perhaps having him boiled with that night's soup, Madame Yum Yum got hold of the chief and made it clear in no uncertain terms that she was getting Santa or else . . .

The Chief immediately pushed Major Dum Dum out of his cabin and ordered him to go up on the back of a Dino Flyer and find Santa or else . . .

Within seconds Major Dum Dum had raced to the Dino
pen and jumped on the back of a high flying Dino
Flyer. The Chief shook his fists for emphasis as
he sent Major Dum Dum on his mission.

No sooner had the Chief turned his back than a giant boulder inexplicably fell out of the sky and plummeted down only to smash but a few inches behind him.

While Major Dum Dum flew away and the Chief shook his fist at him, Santa was with the cave kids as they worked on his magical sleigh. Curious, and trying to avoid hearing another song, Woopy asked Santa to tell them more about Christmas.

As they sat on a log the three cave kids listened to Santa with wide eyes as he spoke to them about the spirit of Christmas and the power of giving to others.

While the children were busy listening to Santa, high up in the sky, Major Dum Dum had spotted them. He dropped a giant net and before they knew it, Santa and the cave kids were trapped.

Major Dum Dum quickly scooped Santa, Woopy, Choo Choo, and Ding Dong up and flew back to the village as fast as he could.

No sooner had Major Dum Dum dumped them in front
of the Chief then they were tossed into a giant
pot of soup. Though the cave kids were scared
there was something about Santa's presence that
gave them hope.

As the Chief lit the fire Ding Dong did a quick set of quite complicated calculations and demised that they would soon start to cook if nothing was done. As jolly as ever, Santa implored the Chief to let them go before he got hurt.

Santa quickly told the cave kids that his plan
included no physical violence of any kind. He
planned to break them out of their boiling pot
predicament by singing a song. Yes . . . a
song. The cave kids were worried, too.

IF YOU THOUGHT SANTA SANG BADLY BEFORE!

Well, the moment Santa opened his mouth, everyone covered their ears. While Santa's voice can be hard to take when he's trying to sound good, when he's trying to sound bad it is absolutely horrendous.

Oh, I've got a song I want to SING!!!
I think you'll like it 'cause it's kind of
a cave man thing.

It's a song you have to sing real real loud.
And I sing it off key because I'm not too proud!

When I sing the chorus, I don't just chirp.
Get ready, here it comes, everybody

BURP!

By the time Santa had reached the final chorus,
the Chief, Major Dum Dum, Madame Yum Yum, and
the other villagers were so distracted by the
pain in their ears that they didn't even notice
when their dinner leapt out of the pot.

Free once again our fearless foursome blazed off
into the forest and headed back to build Santa's
sleigh. They knew they had to move quickly as
the effects of the song would not last long.

As one of the best known toy tycoons in the world, Mr. Horrible took pride in keeping his skin nice and moist. The bananafana facial was part of a weekly ritual that included pounds of aloe vera oil and sleeping with baby kittens taped to his face. Now that Santa's workshop would finally be his, everyone would know about him. Oh, what a glorious thought. No more Santa, more money and all the time in the world to keep his face looking young and flouncy. With all these happy thoughts in his head, Mr. Horrible decided it was time to call Santa's elf and give him the news.

RECIPE FOR ZEE PURRFECT BANANAFANA FACIAL ···

Slice one banana into fifteen of zee little flat slices zat look so cute. Stick zee banana flat slices on zee face so they stick like little glue bunnies Wave your hand in front of zee face so zee wind makes like a blow machine. After fifteen minutes remove and your face will feel five to ten minutes younger.

ENJOY!

But once again Santa's elf dismissed Mr. Horrible as if he were an incorrigible little brat who needed to be sent to the principal's office. Infuriated that Santa had inexplicably survived, Mr. Horrible once more ordered Mr. Mucky back into the plane.

As soon as Santa and the cave kids had gotten back to the site of the explosion they got to work and used the blown up trees to build a slick little sleigh. Santa hopped aboard, said a jolly good bye and was ready to fly home.

Unfortunately, without magic flying reindeer, sleighs tend to stay close to the ground. Santa quickly deduced what the problem was and prepared to give his world famous super duper reindeer call.

Before Choo Choo could stop him Santa belted out a Ho Ho Ho that could be heard for miles and miles. It turns out that when you have a big jolly belly you can Ho Ho Ho really loud.

Though the cave kids were quite concerned that they would soon be surrounded by Dino Dogs on the land and Dino Flyers in the air, Santa remained as jolly as ever, confident that his reindeer would get to him first.

High above the island Mr. Horrible was closing in with supersonic speed. Santa's yell showed up on the instruments and Mr. Mucky instantly relayed the information to Mr. Horrible who pushed a little button that launched a big missile.

Choo Choo was the first to spot Mr. Horrible's G-Seven Three Niner Two Point "0" long range guided missile, which Santa identified with surprising accuracy.

With surprisingly good dexterity, Santa did a last second back bend that saved his life and caused the missile to fly on by without hitting anyone or anything.

After the G-Seven Three Niner Two Point "O" long-range guided missile sailed over Santa, he and the kids looked all around but didn't see another missle headed their way. They took a collective sigh of relief.

Ho Ho Ho, that was close.

Lucky for us it was only Mr. Horrible who found us.

With a prophetic lack of accuracy, Santa jumped to what could only be called a faulty conclusion. However, the kids didn't know what to believe and their faces were portraying emotions ranging from utter relief to fear.

Santa's exhilaration at evading the Seven Three
Niner Two Point "0" long range guided missile
was short lived as a giant boulder plummeted
down from the sky and crashed just inches away
from he and his sleigh.

By the time the Dino Dogs started howling the cave kids were certain that Santa had run out of Christmas spirit and that they were all about to be eaten, boiled, bombed or crushed, depending on who got to them first.

Just when everything looked hopeless, Rudolph appeared and within a matter of moments he and the other reindeer had strapped on their harnesses and hooked themselves to the sleigh. Santa and the cave kids jumped on and they took off right before the Dino Dogs got them.

With the Dino Dogs left behind and the skies seemingly clear, Santa and the cave kids had a moment to breathe, only to have Rudolph spot the horrible toy tycoon's horrible jet on the horizon.

Suddenly the skies were filled with danger as Mr. Horrible and Major Dum Dum flew towards Santa and his sleigh full of friends. Between the boulders and the missiles things looked bleak.

Times were so tense that even the normally unflappable Rudolph was unnormally flapped. Even he had never been in a pickle quite like this one.

Now, reindeer are fast flyers but even they can't outrun missiles or boulders that are being propelled down by gravity at incredible speeds. Rudolph ran through escape plan after escape plan in his mind but no scenario fit. For example, the strudel cake defense* that he'd used in 1752 to fend off a ferocious flock of feral eagles might help with the missile but it left them defenseless against falling boulders. Nothing fit and the more Rudolph racked his brain the more concerned he was that there was no solution.

*The Strudel Cake Defense was made famous in 1567 when the Royal Marksman Squad of the King of Hamburg decided to use Santa's sleigh for target practice. As the arrows were flying up towards him Santa leapt up and in so doing knocked over the Strudel Cake that he was eating. The cake fell over the side and in a mad attempt to retrieve his snack Santa grabbed the reins and dove after the cake. His falling body jerked the reins so hard that Rudolph and the other reindeer were pulled down so quickly that the arrows missed their mark and at the same time Santa grabbed the falling Strudel, leapt back into the sleigh and they flew on in safety.

Major Dum Dum had watched and waited until Santa and the sleigh were right where he wanted them. Then, with all of his cave guy strength, he raised his last giant boulder above his head and hurled it down.

Woopy, Ding Dong, and Choo Choo couldn't believe
the predicament they had gotten themselves into.
Here they were in a magical sleigh flying through
the air with a crazy man, some reindeer and a
bunch of people that wanted to blow them up. But
just when things looked hopeless . . .

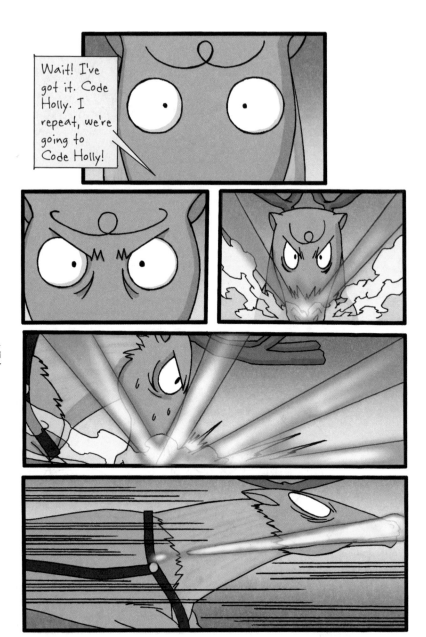

. . . the sleigh shot forward as Rudolph and the other reindeer went into the highest level emergency mode any reindeer had ever mastered. It was known as "Code Holly," or as Santa referred to it: "my favorite way to pass time."

Code Holly was a move so dangerous that it had only been taught to four reindeer, in all of North Pole history. Luckily, it was the four reindeer attached to the sleigh at that very moment.

The giant boulder and the missile closed to within inches of the sleigh, causing Major Dum Dum and Mr. Horrible to celebrate the imminent success of their attacks.

Just as the impossibly loud and impossible to
avoid collision occurred, Rudolph and his
team did a death defying roll and streaked
upwards, causing, against all odds, both the
missile and the boulder to miss.

As soon as they evaded the projectiles, Rudolph
and the other reindeer slowed down back to a
sustainable speed. The sudden exertion caused
by going to such extreme speeds had left them
momentarily exhausted.

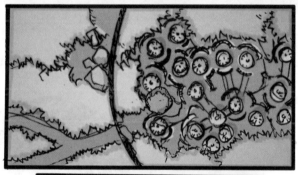

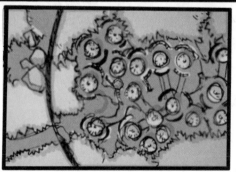

Woopy, Ding Dong, Choo Choo, Santa, Rudolph,
Donner, Comet, and Vixen all looked down and
watched as the giant boulder fell down and
down and down until . . .

MAJOR DUM DUM!!!

Major Dum Dum you either get Santa or when you come down, me cooking you in pot and giving to Madame Yum Yum for din din.

Yum Yum!

. . . it landed right in the middle of the village about one foot behind the chief. Well, the chief was quite surprised but instantly suspected that this falling boulder, like the two or three hundred before it, might have something to do with his assistant.

Worried that Chief Ugga was quite serious, Major Dum Dum turned his Dino Flyer towards a nearby quarry so he could quickly reload with more boulders. Meanwhile, Mr. Mucky had once again closed in upon Santa's sleigh.

Even though they were exhausted, the brave reindeer shot forward again as Mr. Horrible began firing at them. Rudolph and the team had just enough strength left to evade the first round of snowballs and break for a nearby bank of clouds where they hoped to be able to disappear.

Seeing that Santa was headed for the clouds, Mr. Horrible ordered Mr. Mucky to switch to more powerful ammunition: the dreaded megaballs. As anyone who knows about megaball snow cannons knows, they're snowballs that don't look much bigger but they're packed with five thousand times the pressure of normal snowballs and are guaranteed to take magic sleighs down with only a couple of direct hits.

Rudolph continued to lead the team in a series of sharp turns. But, before long Santa took a snowball to the cheek. Knowing that they were about to be shot down again, Santa implored Rudolph to dive into the clouds and, with a burst unseen before or since, Rudolph dove.

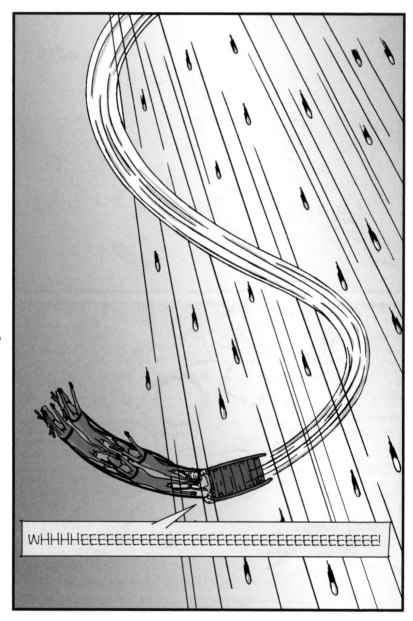

WHHHHEEEEEEEEEEEEEEEEEEEEEEEEEEEEEEEEEEEEEEEEEEEE!

Diving so fast that all Santa could think to do
was go . . . whhheeeeee . . . Rudolph managed
to dodge the barrage of snowballs and, with a
final last plunge, the sleigh darted out of sight
and into a cloudbank where they were suddenly
rendered invisible.

It was at this moment that Major Dum Dum chose to return from the quarry with two giant boulders raised above his head. He searched for the suddenly cloud-cloaked sleigh to no avail. However, when he turned to look around he saw . . .

. . . hundreds, nay thousands, of mega snowballs flying towards him. Major Dum Dum was hit so hard that he and his Dino Flyer were instantly blasted away, however, the two giant boulders were left, momentarily suspended in the air.

At the same moment that Major Dum Dum was blasted away, Mr. Horrible was busy yelling at Mr. Mucky and, though he'd been yelled at a thousand times before, this time two little tears formed in his eyes, momentarily blurring his vision.

The impact of those two boulders colliding with
Mr. Horrible's jet was so great that it is said
you could see the flash and hear the boom all the
way from the back tea room at Mrs. Sally's Happy
Palace in downtown Bora Bora.

Back on Santa's sleigh everybody was happy. They were alive and Christmas was safe from Mr. Horrible for at least another year. Due to the fact that Ding Dong figured that Chief Ugga would need at least 6.5 days to forget what they'd done, Santa invited them to help him on Christmas Eve. Besides, that way, they'd really get filled up with Christmas spirit and share it with everyone on the island.

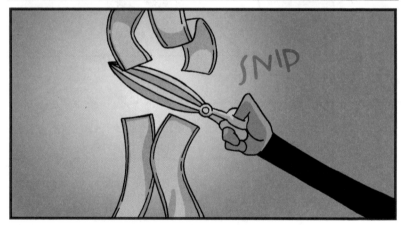

Mr. Horrible and Mr. Mucky had ejected just in
time and ended up dangling fifty-feet above the
ground, stuck in the trees. Side by side they
swung for a few seconds and then Mr. Horrible
gave Mr. Mucky an order and he followed it.

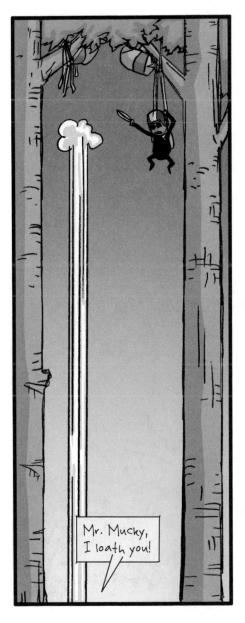

And so ends the adventure of **STONE AGE SANTA**, in which three cave kids learned the power of giving, Major Dum Dum kept missing the Chief with his boulders, Madame Yum Yum never got her chubby furry man dinner, Mr. Mucky finally got a little bit of revenge upon his horrible boss, and Mr. Horrible got a really sore bum from a really high fall. Not a bad little story, all and all. Oh, and yes, Santa learned that even cave kids can become filled with Christmas spirit.

Deck the halls, the book is over . . .
Fa la la la la . . . la la la la
We're just lucky we're not under the clover...
Fa la la la la . . . la la la la
Now it's time to say good-bye...
Fa la la la la, la la la, la la la
Tell all your friends to
give our book a try . . .

Fa la la la la la, la la, la la!

MERRY CHRISTMAS

But wait! Is the story over . . .
What happens to Mr. Horrible and Mr. Mucky who
are now lost somewhere in the Stone Age?

Visit www.stoneagesanta.com to find out!

COMING SOON

The next adventure in the LOST SANTA® series!

Check it out at

www.lostsanta.com